Yasmin

HITMAN'S GIRL

ERIC'S STORY

A DON'T CLOSE YOUR EYES SERIES PREQUEL

LYNESSA LAYNE

A.J. LAYNE

Whatever you do today,
I hope you kill it!

AJ Layne

Lynessa Layne

ONE

Hot water stings my chilled skin and several superficial cuts ignite under the sear of soap I rub over my body. Undulating streams of crimson mix with suds. Pink bubbles swell over the drain. The majority of the blood is not my own.

The Early A.M. Assassin strikes again.

My dive watch reads 3:48 a.m. Five hours and twelve minutes until my first class.

Two hours ago, I'd sent five heinous douchebags to their maker, eliminating a whole pack in one fell swoop rather than hunting them individually as planned. The guy who hired me should send me a bonus.

The white wash cloth, now pink, twists in my hands sore from the garrote, Ka-bar, machete, and lead pipe I'd used as accessories during my impromptu Tang Soo Do matches.

Shampoo burns behind my eyelids. I wince and brace

myself for grateful seconds against the shower wall. The pain means I'm alive. I've come away from another job unscathed. Mostly.

By sunrise, I'll be inside a lecture hall. They'll be the most popular assholes on the morning news and police blotter.

Yellow journalists, sensationalizing the demise of others, now have a macabre massacre to pad their clickbait and ratings. *Would the stupid moniker they'd dubbed me with take credit for this one, too?*

I cut the shower and wipe the mirror with my fist. Tired eyes stare through the fog. Three remained. Three would die. Then, the *Early A.M. Assassin* deserved a much-needed break.

TWO

When you conceptualize a hitman, you probably visualize a ballsy goon or former special operator turned assassin for a fat paycheck; the stereotypical Hollywood imagery of a wet work guy. That's why no one ever investigates me. I hold face-to-face conversations with lead detectives and never rouse suspicion. Educated—dual degrees in Physics and Chemistry, Master's in Forensics, PhD in Criminology —I don't fit Hollywood's bill.

What can I say? An idle mind is the Devil's playground. I did my best to occupy my haunted thoughts. Seems the Devil knows how to play with knowledge too.

By day, I'm a boring, part-time professor at a community-level university. Thanks to the outbreak, the majority of my lectures take me no further than my living room and an excellent internet connection. Handy when nursing hidden aches or licking unplanned wounds.

At times, I lend my credence as a subject-matter-expert to the Prosecution during trials of half-wit killers.

Fascinating thing about the toasted thugs, husbands, and/or gold-digging, insurance-payout wives is… how *stupid* they are. Too passionate, overboard, violent.

Outside the occasional pinch, my preferred modus operandi: one shot, one kill; an untraceable, intricate booby trap; a perfectly-timed, pedal-to-the-metal car accident using a stolen SUV (nobody cuts brake lines anymore—clear messages aren't sent with subtlety these days); even an occasional incendiary explosive is handy when needing evidence destroyed in the process. I take advantage of advanced technology, but believe in being simultaneously adept at analog.

If a client wishes someone whacked overnight, I'm not their guy. Amateurs pull that ignorance. I'm methodical, calculating, analyzing every aspect. My backup plans? A dozen deep. I account for even the most outlandish possibilities.

Stupid is everywhere.

The *Early A.M. Assassin* is a ghost, the bogey man every receiving-end of a contract should fear. No amount of security, bullet-proof whatever, even police or military can save you. After all, they trained me.

Amateurs end up in prison. I end up with six-digits per mark.

To succeed at this vocation, one must abide by a set of rules; an assassin's creed.

Rule #1

No witnesses; includes cameras, people, animals, and anything that could burn you. Eradicate all the above.

Rule #2

Never meet or speak directly with a client. If they discover your name, face, voice, address, or VPN, refer to Rule #1.

Rule #3

Never leave evidence.

Rule #4

Whatever you use to make the hit, destroy it, including clothing and shoes.

Rule #5

Select the moment and situation of *your* choosing, *never* someone else's. There are no time limits on a clean kill with a clean getaway.

Rule #6

Always have an alibi, a rock-solid one.

———

Rule #7

Be willing and able to walk away, at a moment's notice, from everyone and everything. If something feels hinky, bail out, don't look back.

———

Rule #8

Never stay in one residence too long, and always have a safe house / hideout no one knows about.

———

Rule #9

Always pay cash with clean money, not from an ATM or directly from a bank. Banks account for every serial number on and maintain records to help law enforcement nab criminals. No credit or debit cards either—too easy to trace.

———

Rule #10

Only accept payment in untraceable commodities: unmarked precious metals and stones, bearer bonds and the like.

Rule #11

Never get involved. Zero relationships or emotional connections. No conscience with clients, marks, or anyone. Connections WILL be your downfall.

Rule #12

Don't get cocky; sloppiness gets you killed. Always assume the hunter is being hunted.

Rule #13

Always have an exit plan. Know when and how to 'retire' yourself.

Rule #14

***Never* compromise the rules.**

Damn if I didn't break every one of these for the girl. This is where my downfall begins …

THREE

Six Months Ago…

Everyone seeks to reward themselves for a job well done, especially for tough jobs. We overindulge in food, alcohol, drugs, shopping, vacations, etcetera. Addiction is one term colored by many shades of morality. Wet work specialists are no different. My addiction after being paid? Getting no-strings-attached laid.

One-night stands. I hadn't had a girlfriend or relationship longer than forty-eight hours since arriving back on American soil from the sandbox.

I'd unlocked my base housing unit and tripped over someone else's boots. Good thing they took our service weapons when back on base. I'd kicked my bedroom door open to find my wife between our sheets with a townie. The fucktard's shit littered my home: clothing in my dresser, dishes in my sink, toiletries on my vanity, soap in my shower, dick in MY wife.

Fort Bragg, also known as 'FayetteNam', was notorious as sancho central for soldiers and civilians in North Carolina. A unit deployed. Once their flight to the combat zone was wheels up, pull-behind U-Haul trailers streamed onto and off of the base. Spouses either moved into their side-guy's or side-girl's place for the duration of the deployment, or the really brazen ones moved their infidelity into base housing.

When you see wives and husbands running onto the tarmac to hug their soldier home, half of them hold these secrets. The slower they strolled toward the plane, the less loyal they'd been. The ones who didn't hit the pavement to greet their deplaning soldiers, those were the ones about to serve divorce papers.

There was a time when I did my damnedest to be the best husband. I was loyal to a fault, loving, naïve.

That stupid slut stomped my heart repeatedly. The last time, beneath a Jimmy Choo stiletto bought and paid for with my savings, along with scores of lingerie and jewelry I'd never seen beside the intricate pieces I'd brought her back from deployments.

I don't know what I did or didn't do to cause her infidelity. Innocence and decency shot, stabbed, blown-up and burned to ashes, my heart went cold. Not by war. By a woman.

Ever since, though tempted a few times, I'd never allowed a woman inside my head far enough to let her latch on. Holding the grenade of a relationship in my hand too long was bound to result in a destructive explosion. From experience found at the bottom of a liquor bottle and easy women, I'd scienced the safe zone down to a forty-eight-hour window.

Spend more than a weekend with a woman, she'd be your downfall. A roll in the hay on a Ladies' Night with a walk of shame in the morning was the way to go. Physical intimacy and fulfillment without the baggage.

Standards be damned, they weren't always lookers. Hell, for a while there, I admit, I was a chubby chaser. In them, I saw myself—full of regret, depressed, hungry for kindness.

Attention from a put-together, good-looking guy produced ladies all too eager to get me off. I was more than willing to be their romance novel for a night.

Their runway-model-wannabe friends were like racecars, fast, pretty, gone in sixty-seconds, but had insecure, needy and oversexed written all over their stealth bodies. I didn't need or want that reminder of my ex-wife anchoring me down.

Thick girls banged me like a freight train plowing into an eighteen-wheeler stalled on the tracks. Once you got them started, they were hard to slow down. They didn't care that our trysts were a onetime thing. I used them; they used me, and every touch, tickle, taste I gave boosted their self-esteem.

What I didn't expect was the reputation I earned: the go-to guy for women needing a fix. Word traveled. I became a party favor for a growing secret club of hungry women. They sometimes cited girls I'd been with like a testimonial or character reference. I could've printed punch cards to earn a free one-nighter and booked my calendar solid.

The best part about the girls I sacked and shellacked: any of them would be my alibi if ever I asked. Several voiced as much… if they got another night for free.

Good thing because I'd soon cash in a favor ….

FOUR

S trange how one moment, one situation, even one photo can change your entire outlook…

I was driving to a downtown bar for my usual post-mortem decompression when something under a freeway overpass struck me as 'off'. Bright blue like the tarps on roofs after hurricanes and a small flesh-toned something poking out from under the edge.

My palm splayed over the steering wheel. *It's not what you think. You see death all the time. You're imagining it everywhere now. Get laid and get some sleep.*

I continued driving, but a couple of red lights later, I busted an illegal U-turn and drove my Jeep onto the sloping grass beneath the thundering overpass above.

The door slammed behind me as I surveyed the area, uneasy, as if trampling on a serial killer's turf. Trash littered the area. Indigent urine and filth permeated my nostrils as I trudged toward the tarp. A pale, bare foot peeked out from beneath. The casual passer-by wouldn't, *couldn't* notice in the brief seconds of traffic as they whizzed by, but my long-time acquaintance with death forbade me from not noticing. At least I wasn't imagining things.

The closer I got, the more I felt I needed to jet.

911?

Nope. The cops will eventually find this dead hobo. I'm out.

The toes flinched, and I jumped back.

Whoa!

I took several long breaths, willing my nerves out of my queasy stomach.

Alright, dude is alive. Don't be a heartless bastard. Leave a couple of bottles of water and an MRE from the Jeep for him. Having endured the misery of the elements for days and weeks at a time, I felt a kinship to the homeless. The recesses of a haunted mind bred a haven for heroin highs. I didn't use, but I understood why some did. This was probably an overdose.

Carrying the water and MRE back down to the tarp, I froze. I'd expected—well, I don't know what I'd expected. A young woman peeked from beneath the cloth hovel under the tarp.

She tried to scream, but a hoarse cry whispered through what sounded like an injured windpipe.

I lifted the offerings. "I'm not here to hurt you. I promise. I won't hurt you." I kneeled beside the heap. Though she tried to squirm and panic, she made no progress. "I promise," I told her again, lowering my voice, looking around us once more.

My knees hit the dirt beside her. My throat dried. A

blood stain colored the side of the dingy mattress she laid upon. *Hers?* Tears stained and streaked her face. Some old and dry, and new ones followed previous paths down her cheeks.

"I'm gonna lift this up. I'm not gonna hurt you." The tarp crinkled in my hand. The stench of feces and urine slammed my nose so hard my tastebuds took the punch, too. I peeled layers of dirty blankets from her body, the last one stained with her blood. The blanket covered the entry wound, the mattress, her exit wound. I used the bottom of my shirt to retrieve the shell casing of a bullet that rolled away the further I peeled the stained comforters from her nude body.

She whimpered where a sob should've been.

"Shh. Stay calm. We need to get you to a hospital." I had a hard time remaining calm when I saw a long cut across her abdomen. The blood coagulated, but green puss oozed from angry pink flesh. Several stab wounds caked with dried blood and dirt, each appearing as infected as the larger wound.

"Can't. Please."

When my eyes traveled to her face, I saw dark bruising around her neck.

"If we don't get you to a hospital, you're going to die. You've been shot, stabbed, strangled, and—"

She whimpered louder and her bloodstained hand pushed me hard enough I fell onto my ass. A maroon handprint branded the white cotton over my chest.

"Bandages?" she begged through the strain of trying to breathe and cry at once.

"Bandages won't fix this." My hands planted on the dirt. "Look, I don't want any part of what you've gotten yourself into, but I can't leave you to die. I'm calling an ambulance."

"No!" Her whisper broke. "They'll kill me! Eyes everywhere." Every syllable she uttered seemed to shred her esophagus. Tears flowed heavier down her face, dripping onto the mattress. She was likely dehydrated, but tears were a good sign, even if hard to watch.

She was right. Whoever thought they'd killed her would finish if they knew she'd survived. This was *overkill*. How was she still alive?

I looked around and pulled my phone from my pocket.

"No!" She grabbed my wrist holding the phone. "Please leave. Let me die here. I don't want them to come back." The stickiness of damp blood dried between her fingers and my skin.

Recognizing the defeat and fear in her eyes, I said, "I have bandages in my truck." I'd felt that resignation before. Afghanistan. Separated from my team, alone in the middle of a firefight. Surrounded by Taliban. Severely wounded. Abandoned. Certain I wouldn't survive. Willing to die alone rather than found and tortured by demented sycophants. I didn't know who her Taliban was, but I'd be damned if I left her here and on my conscience.

"I know a guy who can patch you up," I insisted. "No one will know. He's the guy I go to when I get jacked up."

"I—I can't. Risky."

"Look, girl. It's a miracle you're alive. That I even

spotted you. If you don't get treated right away, you'll be dead in a day or two, hopefully before the bugs start eating you alive. I'm not taking no for an answer. A Ranger never leaves a man behind." I pushed back into a kneeling stance.

My team took two days, but they came back for me. Not a rescue mission, a recovery mission—for my body. They were as shocked as me when I wasn't quite dead, though damn close.

"Brace yourself. This will hurt." I ripped the band-aid and at once shoved my arms beneath her bloody back and knocking knees. My face remained painfully neutral, though furious anger raged when seeing this wounded animal in the light of day without the shitty coverings they'd thrown over her.

She tried to help, tried holding my neck, but I shifted her, so her head lolled against my chest.

"If I get to kill the asshole who did this to you, bonus." I hurried up the slope and opened the back door behind my driver's seat.

She cried and winced when her wounds touched the leather, some splitting open again. Without the shade of the overpass and tarp, I saw now a deep red bruise on her cheek, lips puffy and split.

I uncapped a bottle of water and helped her drink. The sound of her gulps made my throat hurt for her. She smelled like death had used the restroom on her. I'd have to replace the upholstery. A cadaver dog could sniff a body if I didn't. Poor girl. Water dribbled down the sides of her mouth, but she drank until the bottle was empty.

"You couldn't kill the men who did this to me," she rasped when I tossed the bottle on the floorboard. "You'd have to have a death wish."

"Maybe I do." I unrolled a sleeping bag and covered her. "Have a death wish, that is."

FIVE

Twenty minutes later, I steered the Jeep down my former Ranger medic's driveway, catching him up over the phone like an EMS driver with a critical victim.

"I don't know her vitals. I didn't take them. Didn't think about it. She was talking. I got her to drink a bottle of water." The girl didn't make a peep the whole drive. She might've died en route.

Barklay rushed up to the Jeep as soon as I cleared the last bend. After we hung up our digis, we became beer buddies trying to figure out what to do with our lives civilian side. When I got into wet work, Barks was working fast food, depressed, on the verge of suicide. I brought him into the fold and paid his debts with my first hit. Got him the land and modular cabin with my second. Loyalty matters.

"She's unconscious," he said, fingers to her ankle. "Weak pulse. Let's get her inside."

I climbed into the backseat, and he took her feet while

I hoisted her arms. There was something eerie about holding the dead weight of a living person.

Barks coughed over a gag. "Dude, where did you find this girl? In a sewer? You've slummed it before, but I believe this is rock bottom."

"Funny," I muttered through gritted teeth as we carried her inside to his shower/tub combo.

Barklay left to get an IV and syringe to sedate her. I held the shower head away from the girl until the water was warm. She didn't flinch under the spray or the needle he put into her arm. Blood, dirt, shit, piss and water drained around our feet while medicine pushed from his thumb through the syringe into her veins.

We set about scrubbing her clean before scrubbing ourselves clean enough to stitch her wounds.

"That's not good," Barklay said under his voice. I followed his gaze to the wound on her abdomen. "Let's get her on the table. You're assisting. Then, you're bleaching my bathroom." The tub stained with a nasty ring. "Where'd you find her?"

I filled him in while he sterilized and sutured. I stood by with supplies on demand. He removed two bullets, stitched half a dozen knife wounds, all infected, then cut away layers of necrotic skin around her abdomen.

"Was there a baby anywhere nearby?"

My attention snapped to his masked face. "Baby?" My brow furrowed.

"Someone cut a baby from her body. This …" He used a pair of clamps and pulled a nasty, bloody blob of a thing from the opening he'd made in the old cut. "… Is placenta. And an enormous source of infection. See this? Umbilical cord."

Not much made me green, but this made me rush to the toilet. While I flushed, I heard him snort to himself. Every snip, snip, snip of her black skin made me sick all over again. A baby. I had to go back.

I forearmed my mouth and pulled a mask on again. "Is she going to live?"

"Not sure. The damage and infection are extensive. Her abdomen was going green, man. All I can do is put her on high dose antibiotics, keep this saline drip going, and stitch her up. I've cut away all I can. Now it's up to time and fate, but she's a fighter to have lasted this long. Someone wanted her dead."

"Maybe the father?" I asked.

He shrugged and shook his head. "Looks like the work of at least three. Not just one."

He was right. She'd said *men*.

"She a pro. Branded." He lifted her hair away from her neck. A tattoo marked her behind the ear.

"Shit." I swallowed and stared at Barks. He nodded, knew. "It's Russian."

"You sure know how to pick a fight." Barklay tossed his tools into the sink. "Hope you know what you've gotten yourself into."

SIX

Over the next two weeks, I pulled three jobs, gave eight lectures, visited four bars, but found little interest in my normal after-hours head-clearing. The women on my roster pestered me for a good time. I gave them what they were looking for, but my head wasn't in the game.

I'd gone back to the overpass twice and searched in all directions for a baby. The good news: no sign of an infant. The bad news: no sign of an infant.

Scenarios of her suffering seared my mind as I cased the scene of her crime more like a cop than a killer. Too bad I couldn't call the cops on this. Too many insiders.

How far along was she? Maybe they'd cut a fetus from her that was too young to survive? Maybe the baby was dead? Maybe … maybe I should stop thinking about her and her baby.

But I couldn't. If she'd been trafficked, her baby would be a hot commodity, too. The idea was more repulsive than the state I'd found her in. What was *her* name?

Despite Barks' warning, I found myself visiting homeless encampments and shelters asking about a pregnant prostitute who might've recently gone missing. Did anyone know anything about a baby? If I'd had a picture of the girl to show people, I might make progress.

After too many hours of radio silence from Barks, I drove over to his house. *Had the girl died? Was he ghosting me, afraid of my reaction? It wasn't like I'd attached to her or something.*

WTF?

Barklay's truck parked in the drive, but he wasn't answering the door. After the warning he'd given about the Russians, my first thought was they'd found her, killed him, knew I'd been asking questions.

I ripped the gun from my ankle holster and jogged around the back of the house to find him sitting on the porch swing with a cup of coffee. My footfalls paused mid-step, and the gun lowered to my side. The girl lounged on a wicker love seat, staring out over his back garden koi pond. Wow! *Not the girl on death's door I'd expected.*

"Hey, Ghost, how's it hangin'?" Barks asked, unfazed by my weapon.

"Ghost?" The girl tilted her head. She wasn't fazed either.

"Yeah, my bro's callsign in Afghanistan was Ghost… The Ghost of Khowst. The enemy could never find him when he got sent on solo recon missions taking out high-value targets." He looked at me. "This is Emily, by the way. Emily Aguado."

"Ah. Nice to officially meet you, Emily." My attention

diverted to her healing face. The bruises faded into simple shadows. Without swelling distorting her features, she was quite pretty, natural, wholesome. Nothing like a used-up pro. She must've had a higher station than a street corner.

"Nice to meet you, too … uh, do I call you Ghost?" she asked, uncertain. Barks didn't say a word, which I appreciated.

"It's best you do," I told her. "I'm glad to see you're up and about. How are you feeling?" I tucked the weapon back at my ankle.

"A little better than the last time you saw me." Her voice was strong, whole in pitch, healed. We stared at each other for an awkward, silent moment. "Thank you." She dropped her gaze. "For saving me." *Though I hate living every minute* her crystalline eyes said when she looked back up at me.

"You're welcome," I replied, kindred to her in more ways than one. Unable to withstand the odd guilt of forcing her to live after her trauma and losing her child, I went inside to get a cup of joe from the carafe Barks made. He always found good stuff. Expensive. Imported. "What's on the menu today, good sir?" I trailed through the screen door.

"Kona—and not that ten percent cheap ass shit that's blended with Arabian throat grinder garbage—one-hundred percent Hawaiian Kona. Had an old buddy of ours pick up a case for me in Kauai while he's stationed in paradise," Barks proudly proclaimed.

"Nice." I stuffed two packages into my cargo pants pockets of the twenty-three left in the case.

"You're welcome," Barks grinned. He knew. He always knew. I much more leisurely exited onto the back porch now that I had a little sip of caffeine heaven pulsing through my veins.

"So, Emily …" I inhaled the steamy aroma with an unnatural pleasure. "What's your story?" I stared into the woods beyond the neatly manicured Japanese garden and koi pond as I waited for a response; always scanning, always vigilant. Take nothing for granted. Silence, except for the occasional sip of coffee, birds singing and the faint squeaks from the porch swing, owned the air.

"Four years ago, I was in my freshman year of college, walking across the campus parking lot, excited for a party that weekend. The boy I'd liked asked me to be his date. I was texting him when I saw these three guys in leather jackets and track suits leaning against a van. I thought it was strange, considering it was early May in Miami and they didn't look like students. Next thing I know, my phone flies out of my hand, two of those guys grabbed me, threw me in the sliding door of a Mercedes delivery van, and take off.

"Before I could fight, I felt a pinch on my neck and things went fuzzy. That's the last thing I remember before waking up in a nightmare."

"So, you were abducted by human traffickers."

"Is that what you call them? Your description is much more civil than what I came to know them as."

"And what's that?"

"Evil. Pure evil." Emily's eyes glossed over; her arms crossed as she went to another place in her mind. She spun her legs to sit up, and dipped her head into her hands, tears dripping through her fingers. All the cold blood in my arteries boiled warm. I wasn't naïve to the trade. I'd just never been involved directly or known 'the commodity' for rent or sale. From time to time, I took out targets; mostly Cuban and Mexican traders wanted dead by rival competition.

"Which cartel?" I asked off-hand, praying Barks and I were wrong about the tattoo on her neck.

"Not a cartel." She sniffled. "Russian mob." My stomach soured.

"No shit? Here? Thought they were only a problem in major cities up north."

"Where do snowbirds fly for winter? If half their clientele leaves for Florida, you gotta go where the customers go.

"They came to *Tampa* because I escaped the bordello in Miami and hopped a Greyhound headed anywhere else. I skipped one stop, but being big pregnant, I had to pee really bad, so I took a chance and got out in Tampa. I was in the bathroom when they found me and dragged me to that awful spot under the bridge. They wanted ..."

She choked with a painful sob. "They wanted my ba-ba—"

She barely screeched the word. "*Baby.*" The sound forced harder through her lips than the day I'd met her. "They're here. And they're ruthless. They don't care about anyone or anything. They'll kill anyone without hesitation. I've seen it. I've felt it."

"They thought they'd killed you," I reiterated my first impression at the overpass.

"I must've passed out when they shot me. Thought I

was dead. Woke up in so much pain, covered in blood and trash. My baby was gone from my belly. I tried to save her," she lamented. "I tried to get us as far from them as I could."

"Do you know why they wanted your baby? Isn't it bad for prostitutes to get pregnant?"

"Ghost!" Barklay chastised my candor.

"No," she said. "It's a fair question. The leader wanted a baby. Said his wife wanted to start a family without ruining her figure. We weren't all for sale, you see. They kept some of us in a private harem until he tired of us."

I blinked. Hard. Barks got up for a refill and disappeared behind the screen door. I heard his coffee mug smack the sink too hard.

"It's his?" I asked what I didn't want to.

She nodded, her chin quivering. "But it's mine! She's mine! She grew in my body! She kicked me from the inside. In the last few weeks, I could see her toes and tickle her feet when she'd press them against my skin." The saddest smile lit her bleary eyes. "I patted her bottom when she'd push too hard next to my ribs. I sang to her. Read to her. She … was my world. A bright spot in the darkest place imaginable. I couldn't lose her or let him give her to his wife.

"When I asked if they'd let me nurse her after she was born, he said that his wife was going to bottle feed her and if she wanted more children by me, they'd keep me. If she thought the baby was ugly, she'd sell both of us and they'd try again."

"How long before I found you did that happen?"

"Three days."

"Tough girl," Barks said as the screen door slammed behind him. He took his perch on the swing again.

"Very," I agreed, though sick to my stomach and filled with rage. "You were from Miami when they took you, and they kept you in Miami all along?" Head scratch. "Were you in the system, or something?" I knew kids disappeared from the foster system through political channels. Anyone who tried to stop or expose the crimes ended up creatively suicided.

"No. They knew where I lived and made sure I knew they'd kill my parents or sell my mother. They'd stalked me for weeks. They do it with all the victims that might be missed." She looked down at her nails. "I didn't get to meet my baby, but I miss her. I can't imagine how my parents feel wondering what happened to me. I miss them so much. I wish I could tell them I'm alive, but it's too dangerous."

I checked my dive watch. "Welp—"

Barks said, "Nope."

"I've got somewhere to be," I continued. "Thanks for the coffee." I looked into her haunted eyes. "Thank you for sharing your story. I'm sorry for everything that's happened to you. You're in the best hands."

Barks excused himself. "I'm gonna walk him out."

I shouldn't have looked over my shoulder. Something dimmed in her face when I walked away. My throat was thick, and I cleared my airway multiple times. Barks fast-walked beside me.

"Are you crazy?" he hissed.

I yanked at the door to the Jeep. "Nope. For the first time in a long time, I'm human. Don't make a big deal of it. I'll check in." I slammed the door on his protest and started the vehicle.

"What if you die?"

"You know the drill. If I die, I go out guns blazing with my boots on."

SEVEN

I drove... and drove... and drove. No particular destination, just cruising southbound on County Road 39 to think things through. Three hours later, I was in Naples, and on fumes, so I pulled off the major thoroughfare to fuel up.

I checked my watch – a little after 1 p.m. I could be in Miami in a couple of hours. I was already three-fifths of the way there. Letting out a deep breath as my gas cap spun off and the nozzle went in, I figured I ought to at least investigate the lay of the land, get a feel for what I'd be up against.

Worst case, I could pull an easy lay to make up for the opportunity I passed on while investigating crimes I shouldn't. Besides, if I got back on my game, maybe temptation would fade, and I'd get my groove back.

I had to find that baby. What if the baby wasn't to the wife's liking?

I hardly noticed the gas nozzle still in my grip, overflowing the tank until I heard the splash on the pavement. Some random guy rolled up to the pump behind me, hopped out of his jacked up 4x4, cigarette still hanging from his lips. Nothing against smokers, but I have a problem with dying a stupid *immediate* death because some asshole didn't pass high school science. *The vapors ignite and go boom, you effin' moron.*

I stalked over and ripped the cig from his face, smashed the cherry under foot, and gave him the 'I *will* kill you' mean mug. Redneck bravado flamed from his vocal chords. One flash of the chrome .45 I eased from the small of my back as I booted back to the Jeep, and dude figured there were better gas stations to blow up with his reckless habit.

He backed out and hit the street as fast as he thundered in. I've been told there's something in a killer's eyes that tells you he's not bluffing. I got the feeling deep down that I'd be face-to-face with a Russian outfit with eyes full of that 'something' like mine soon.

I grabbed a bag of ice, a case of water and a big bag of gator jerky to keep me company on Highway 41 through the Everglades, and put the rubber on the road. As soon as I hit Hialeah, the error in timing was glaringly obvious.

Time hack—4:35 p.m. Rush hour in Miami. Fantastic. My thirty-minute drive to South Beach wouldn't have turned into an hour and a half if I hadn't stopped. Regardless, I was in the Miami-Dade metro. If the Ruskies had any kind of influence on the drug and prostitution trade, SoBe was prime real estate for top dollar clients who wanted top quality whores and top quality blow. The Moscow mules weren't stupid.

They ran their mob like a corporation. They were

careful. Even though they had cops and politicians on the payroll, they knew business would suffer if their brand of brutality was out in the open, especially at the playground of celebs and tycoons. They also realized with their smaller numbers, alliances with the Italians were a necessity, though they kept their sights on taking over the entire area as soon as they had the strength in numbers to do so.

No, they reserved their worst conduct for the cheap rent districts and dark alleys. I'd stick out like a sore thumb in the barrios. South Beach was much easier to blend in. Anonymous. Tourist with a beach mobile. The logical starting point for my intel gathering. I pulled into a truck stop on the outskirts to shower, change into the chic casual attire I kept in the Jeep for bar hopping, dashed some high-end cologne on the hot spots, slicked the hair, and continued east.

It didn't take long to glean my first taste of the Russians' influence. I parked the truck by the beach walk, trotted across the street to one of the art déco bars & grill, and was seated at a two-top by the sidewalk. I'd barely taken a sip of my Modelo when a Cuban kid about twelve years old approached from the sidewalk with an ulterior motive in his eye.

If you've traveled internationally, you know the look. The locals' 'everybody's got an agenda' 'let's make a deal' look in the eye. Sure enough, the kid looked around casually and leaned on my table.

"Hey mister, you lookin' to score? Pretty girls? Primo green? Maybe a walk on the wild side?"

"Maybe."

"Cool, brah. When you're done with dinner, cruise

over to the Back Bar two blocks that way," he worked me. Though he was Cuban, vices don't happen without permission or commission of the criminal organization in charge of the turf. Kid was earning scratch pulling customers as discreetly as a twelve-year-old had the gumption to. At least I hadn't had to ask a single question. Questions make you suspect, a fool, or a rookie undercover cop, hence the risk in my asking around the homeless camps.

The locals know how to score. Asking questions makes you kryptonite. Nobody wants to be anywhere near you. The more powerful the crime boss, the further the distance. Same with hitmen.

Ten-dollar bottle of beer, thirty-dollar Mahi, and the only thing on the menu worth the money was the flan. I tipped my waitress, gulped the swill and shuffled the sidewalk in the general direction the kid had pointed. Sure enough, two blocks west of the SoBe strip, there was a non-tourist local dive called the 'Back Bar'. Somewhere between seedy and needy. Not like New York, where the girls are sleazy and hovering around the place. Not on open display. I cruised up to the door, and the kid was there nodding approval to the doorman tucked just inside the entry.

"Ten bucks," the doorman's gruff voice demanded with a Russian accent, cigar in his cheek, and the personality of a manhole cover.

I handed the man a ten, and the kid led me deeper into the dimly lit joint. The kid led me past the bar and through a door. Yet another doorman inside that doorway barked, "Twenty bucks." Wow, the dynamic duo, thirty bucks, and I still didn't even have a beer in my hand.

The kid took me to a cocktail table in a dark corner with faux leather seating, pulled the curtain almost closed, and asked for my drink order.

"Modelo… *unopened*," I quipped.

The kid caught on that I'd caught on and winked his silent opinion that I'd made a wise choice. "Coming right up, mister."

Before the beer was served, an attractive young woman entered through the curtain to the small round booth, sat, scooted and cozied up to me, an arm around my neck, and her other hand on my shoulder. Her mouth was so close to my ear, I smelled the vodka on her breath. *Femme fatale fixer.*

"Darling," she tugged my earlobe with, "what's your pleasure?" her Russian accent cooed into my neck.

"What's on the menu?" I played along with a smile. "I'm somewhere less sophisticated than caviar, but don't serve me soup du jour."

"Do you prefer Grade A American beef, Greek Gyro, Cuban sandwich, Korean barbecue, French dip, or maybe some tender young veal?" The temptress referred to nationalities and ages. "We have some amazing desserts to go with the main course. Perhaps a lemon custard tart with powdered sugar on top?" *Cocaine.* "Caramel drizzle?" *Heroin.* "Mint leaf garnish?" *Marijuana.*

"How about a Cuban with mint garnish on the side?" I selected.

"Ah, the local flavor. Not into exotic tastes, handsome?" The vixen tried to upsell.

"Like I said, caviar is a little above my price range, *bella*."

"Suit yourself, but if you'd like to upgrade next time, just ask for Olga, dollface. I always select the finest cuts of meat and the freshest desserts at market price," she teased, fingernails caressing my jawline as she rose and exited as gracefully as she'd entered.

A few minutes later, Olga returned and gave the come-hither finger roll, beckoning to follow her. She led me through yet another door and down a hallway into the adjacent building, up a set of stairs and down another hallway to the last door on the left. She opened the door, and inside waiting were two Cuban girls, maybe college age, lounging on a plush, oversized sofa covered in merino wool skins. In front of them sat a neatly arranged silver platter with a dessert bowl of weed, a pipe, and a tamper.

She tallied my bill and held out a hand to receive payment. Five hundred dollars. Two hundred per girl (Cuban 'sandwich') and a C-Note for the ganja. I ponied up, thanked Olga, and closed the door. The sound of her stilettos clacked back down the hallway. I'll give it to the Russians. Their high-end bordello was definitely classier than what I expected, but I was quite certain their other establishments weren't posh or proper like Olga's. I wondered to myself if she'd been a working girl who worked her way up with favors, or merely a vested and more polished *member* of the mob who had the pizazz to sweet talk and upsell their wares to a more discerning clientele.

"*Hola Señor.*" The Cuban cuisine welcomed me into the dining room. These girls were not your typical street trash back-alley whores or drive-thru pump-and-dump backseat candy. They were pretty girls, like Emily. Had they once been part of the private harem?

They claimed to be eighteen and nineteen and gave names that were likely assigned to them by their madam. They patted the middle of the large 'love' seat, enticing me to get comfortable between them, which I did, and as one girl retrieved the goodie tray for me, the other popped a cork and poured champagne for the three of us. I'd chosen the least-intoxicating 'dessert' and the most 'local' main course on the menu intentionally.

Cuban girls knew the lay of the land in Miami. Someone likely separated them from family upon arrival in Florida, having escaped from the Castro regime and naively being taken in by 'good Samaritan' traffickers before they even got their bearings on the mainland.

They spoke passable English, enough to cover the wants and needs of their clientele, but not enough to really blend in anywhere but Miami. Fortunately, I spoke fluent Spanish from my time growing up in San Miguel de Allende in Guanajuato, Mexico with my expat parents.

Our dialects didn't exactly match up, but conversation was much easier with these girls in Spanish, and they livened up as soon as I put them at ease—a *Guero* speaking fluent Spanish, flush in cash, suave yet genuine, to a beautiful Latina, is a sugar daddy waiting to happen. A way out.

They exchanged a competitive look like the wheels turned in their enamored heads faster than they could get my clothes off. I admit, taking one (or two) for the team, to gather intel had never been so... enjoyable.

I don't do whores because I don't buy sex. This rare departure was exactly what I needed to pause my incessant thoughts of Emily and her baby. I needed to get the 'lay' of the land myself.

Two hours with 'Nina' and 'Chiquita', combined with the haze of some of the best green I've ever smoked, left me relaxed, sated, and spent. Between tricks, taking turns, and switching positions, the girls slipped in simple conversation. They filled me in using Spanish and I wondered whether Olga and her crew knew their language as well as I did.

On clouds of THC, tidbits of information flowed about the organization, what they knew, and a handful of names. Lower-level guys who ran the business fronts like this one. Pieces of the pie that I could put together for a bigger picture, in time. Amazing what a woman will tell you when you're in the throes of passion and focused on stimulating *her*.

"Did one of you say your name was Emily?" I asked in Spanish.

"No." One giggled at the other. "Emily doesn't work this scene anymore. We all came in together. Volkov liked her green eyes."

"They're not green. They're golden," the other said.

"They're mixed. Sometimes green. Sometimes golden. Volkov liked that, so they put her in the penthouse. We don't see her anymore."

This was a start, at least, and the most pleasurable interrogation I'd ever induced. I thanked the girls and kissed them *adios* with promises I'd return, which I had no intention of doing, leaving them with false hope of their *conquistador* swooping in to rescue them.

Perhaps, indirectly, I'd eliminate their captors and provide an unguarded door to escape? That would take time, though, and my primary mission didn't include side jobs. I needed to find out where the child was, if she was still alive, and how to get her out of the mob's grasp.

Hostess Olga was all smiles at the end of the hallway. When I approached, she looped her arm elbow-in-elbow with mine.

"So, were our ladies to your liking?"

"Yes, quite," I affirmed.

"Perhaps next visit, you'd enjoy the unique and tantalizing touch of Russian girl? A former gymnast? With incredible flexibility?" she enticed.

"A certain hostess extraordinaire?" I side-eyed her with a smirk. Maybe Olga was the key to getting into the penthouse.

"Mmm… you seem like man who has stamina to keep up with vigorous, how you say… playmate?"

"I might, indeed." I kept the option open with Olga, as much curious as tactical. This chick likely had more information I needed than the working girls, though she seemed selective in the clients she'd actually lower herself back into the trade for. Yep, she must've worked her way up. Probably raised by a good family, but after gymnastics left her behind, she resorted to the oldest trade to pay the bills back in Mother Russia, and made a name for herself in the organization. Earned her way out of the back rooms to the front office.

"My card, should you be available during your stay in

Miami," Olga suggested, slipping a business card into my pocket. "Call me." She kissed my neck, depositing lipstick on my collar. This girl was good. Marking territory that wasn't yet hers, ensuring no other woman would so much as approach me if this shirt remained. Bet this chick had caused a few dozen divorces back in babushka land.

I had to be careful, though. She may be feeling me out and trying to peg my game as much as I was trying to infiltrate hers. Counter-intelligence? Never let your guard down.

EIGHT

I got to work researching names, obtaining cell numbers and addresses for the handful of mobsters the Cubanas divulged. Sweat beaded down my back as I concentrated on the task. Russian techies weren't who you wanted a digital trail left behind for.

For days, I hopped seedy motels using background-check site subscriptions, VPN, fake email addresses—different email addy and membership for each site and search. Sprinkle a few dozen false identities with legitimately viable ID's, a handful of elected county coroners eager for a cash bump in their salaries, and recorded serial numbers of every bill you bribed them with to keep them from giving up the Ghost, and I was in business.

I paid them better than the cops did. Over the past five years, I'd amassed quite a few alter egos and disguises. It's good to be a state-approved general contractor, city building inspector, crime scene photographer, or health inspector.

I drove around town looking for signs of illicit activities and collecting tricks of the trade. A productive shopping day yielded excellent results. Clothing, footwear, spy shop gear, prosthetics, a little makeup and cheap cologne, and a few health code violations. I was ready to pull a fast one or two on the mob. I downloaded and printed off city inspection forms, bought a cheesy metal clipboard with storage and beat it up a little to lend legitimacy.

I bought a 1986 Honda Accord for five-hundred dollars at a rent-a-wreck lot to finish out the disguise, then littered the car with paperwork, crumpled fast food bags and random business cards from a local pub wall. No one would be duped by a 'city employee' making enough to afford my jacked and stacked Jeep rollin' on 35s with a snorkel intake.

Within a week, I gleaned enough information on the Russians to figure out a couple of neighborhoods they were operating out of. There were sure to be a couple of code violating buildings to inspect that housed illegal activities and more members of the crew to dig the dirt on. The more dossiers I put together, the deeper I dug into their lairs, the higher chance of success in the overarching endeavor.

Russians don't play well with snoops. City officials? They either try to grease the wheels monetarily, make threats, or tell you to come back later. Nobody cast a side-eye when I rolled up like Mister Rogers in the Honda. In addition, I'd planned my alias thoroughly. The numbers on the business cards I'd printed went straight to Barks and a couple other close confidants who were very convincing 'city employees' on my payroll. Soon, the low-level Ruskies were satisfied that I was legit, and allowed me back to 'do my job'.

I found 'minor violations' of city building codes, recommended fixes and local contractors who could 'help get things up to code'. Nothing that would raise eyebrows or garner too much attention as serious. Timelines to avoid fines interested the grass roots mobsters to get me and the city out of their hair as soon as possible so they could carry on with their vice dens. Of particular note was the fact that every one of their establishments, upon my delayed return, showed zero evidence of prostitution, drug trade, illegal gambling or nefarious activity.

A handshake, a goofy nerd smile, and a push of my black-rimmed BCGs (Birth Control Glasses) from tip to bridge of my nose, and the bottom tier mobsters were relieved to 'pass' inspection.

Within a couple of weeks, I'd hit all the street-level places of business. I wasn't naïve, though. There had to be hideouts, safe houses, upper-level addresses to consider. Fortunately, after the collapse of the condos in Florida, codes changed, and laws passed that may grant me entrance into the expensive dwellings where I was sure to find Volkov.

One of the building 'supers' slipped, and I hit pay dirt when I overheard him back-and-forthing with an enforcer as he scrutinized my business card, inspection forms, and clipboard after patting me down.

'Volkov'. What little Russian I'd picked up from interactions with the Russian army in Syria came in handy. I picked out keywords: "Boss" "Volkov" "Not happy"

"Better fix" "Move merchandise" "Get rid of / make disappear".

They wanted my nuisance out of their lives before the big boss got pissed and dealt with them... and me. Even mobsters knew if they land on the city's radar, things get ugly for them — more so with the big boss than with the city bureaucrats. Take initiative and deal with the pain in the ass so the boss doesn't deal with you.

Now I had a location and confirmation. I needed to know who Volkov was. Maybe someone in my network of middlemen, providers, and fixers would recognize the name or have had dealings with the Russians and a little more data to sift through. At the end of my resources, I called a guy I'd hung out with at Bagram. Jase Taylor, a former SEAL.

"Nah, man," Jase said. "Never heard that name, but I know a guy who might. I'll get back to you tomorrow."

The moment his number hit my screen; the phone glued to my ear. Jase got straight to the point, no pleasantries. "The guy I'm working for has a dossier on Volkov, no photos. Former Stasi, Russian secret police." 'Cagey' was the word he used to describe the elusive don of the 'Miami Moscovas'. If only I could get a photo...

"Thanks, Jase."

A full calendar page passed since I'd left the Tampa area to reconnoiter the Russians. I missed the creature comforts of home, especially considering the pompous-ass pretentious pricks and bitches around the Miami beach vicinity. I much preferred my groovy St. Pete surroundings and people. No puffery... unless you count over-the-top fish tales from the local anglers.

I gained as much intel as I could without becoming suspicious or being followed. Any longer, and people would ask questions. Time to bail out.

I stowed the Honda in a storage unit on the west side of Hialeah, then caught a cab back to my Jeep I'd left in a parking garage a few blocks from SoBe. Never take the same roads. Predictability equals death. Along I-75, I screened the rear-view for tag-alongs, but after an hour found nothing, so I relaxed a little.

Fortunately, we weren't in high season for tourists and theme park traffic yet, so most road warriors were truckers headed to Naples and destinations north to Tampa.

A convertible full of beach bunnies were about all that caught my eye; two in the backseat lifted their bikini tops as they passed, then granted a few truckers an eyeful. Nice. Yet another reason to love Florida.

I arrived in Treasure Island, my primary residence, did my usual neighborhood sweep and gave a few neighborly waves before pulling into the driveway and tucking the Jeep into garage bay number three around back, invisible from the street.

More rules: Never leave your vehicles in the open for potential hunters, or police, to pull your tag number. Keep the sprinklers, lights, and TV on a timer—HGTV at 7:30 on weeknights. Don't choose the sports channel; neighborhood sports fans may take note and strike up a conversation.

No man's man is going to open a conversation on interior design or *Love It or List It*. Park a cheap car in the visitors' side drive. In my case, a beat-up '93 F-150 with a few patches of rust and a flat-bottom John boat trailer'd up. Nothing break-in worthy. Add a couple cheesy Floridian gnomes in the garden. Toss an *I'd rather be fishing* sign above the doorbell. Season with random accoutrements that scream 'regular guy' and sprinkle 'wifely' décor to throw off suspicion that you're anything but just the generic guy next door.

And NEVER bring anyone to the place you sleep, where you're vulnerable. I'd fit in here for the past couple of years as a 'telemarketer', a career choice that nobody really wants to know too well. Boring, run of the mill. Nobody asks for your help.

You don't have 'fix-it' skills, you can't get them a deal on something from work, and even the boat screams freshwater fishing hobby. Only lower to lower middle-income people go to a lake to fish in Florida. Everyone else saltwater fishes. My cover life was thoroughly planned, innocuous and dull. I'm not the guy you invite over for barbecues or wanna swill beer with at the local watering hole. Uninteresting. Safe. Solitary. Sometimes I hated that.

I tossed the junk mail on the kitchen counter and looked out over the canal.

What to do? I felt better knowing a little more about the 'Miami Moscovas', but the information didn't allay my trepidation for pulling off the job.

My phone buzzed. On the other end, Jase told me to meet him at his place in the woods east of Tampa in a couple of hours. He had some info to discuss, and a potential lead for help with my 'home improvement project'.

Jase was interesting. We'd become fast friends in the Middle East, never without a topic, and never without a laugh. He was a bit off the norm, though. After a stint in Leavenworth for killing the wrong person in Afghanistan, he'd moved to Florida, started a bar band, made association with shady characters, and even shadier women. He was more than met the eye, and I was sure he was in business with elements of Tampa's criminal underground. Translation: he had connections. Of eccentric note was the 'pet' 12-foot alligator, Torro, he kept in the pond behind his house. SEALs. They're weird.

I pulled up in my old F-150, recently detached from the boat trailer, and gave a rap on the doorjamb to the pre-agreed rhythm that kept a visitor from taking twelve-gauge buckshot to the torso through the door. After a couple incidents had the Mormon boys peddling their bicycles as fast as their highwater black slacks allowed, even they knew this place was off-limits.

A quick look around the property from the doorway, Jase pulled me in by my collar. "Let's go out to the dock."

On his way through his kitchen, Jase deposited his cell phone in the oven, me following suit en route out the back door.

"You sure about this?" He climbed inside a Gator UTV.

I got in beside him and gave him a look that asked, *are you serious?*

He chuckled under his breath, started the vehicle, and shifted gears. "Hope she's worth it. You go an' fall in love?"

"No!" I shouted over the engine and bugs splatting the windshield. "I barely know her!"

The tires of his side-by-side spit mud once we arrived before the five-acre pond. When we got out, Jase retrieved two dead chickens from the back, noosed their necks, and fastened them to a couple of empty dock posts.

"Torro's feeding time," Jase said. "Don't hang too close to the edge. He gets a little nippy when he hasn't eaten for a few days."

"Duly noted." I leered down at the water, then chose to sit on an old, wrought-iron bench facing the end of the dock. Jase handed me a Ziplock full of puppy food, opened one of his own, and tossed kibble into the water for the fish.

"I know a guy."

"Just *one*?" I tested.

"He has very capable associates, but prefers to work alone for this kind of job. Goes by Mr. White. No first name. He's a pro. Very thorough. Experienced."

"Mr. White? Like in *Reservoir Dogs*?" I chuffed to myself, tossed puppy food.

"Hmph." Jase's head tilted. "Yeah. I never thought of that. Guess so."

"So, you think *two* guys can pull off a project of this magnitude? What, is he some kinda James Bond?" I turned to Jase with a concerned expression, all humor gone.

"He works for a power player with a lot of weight behind him, Ghost. He's no slouch. You're good. He's better. He's so meticulous, he has a dossier on *you*."

"He can't be that good. I've never heard of him. Why would he have a file on me?"

"This dude has a file on all the movers and shakers in the underworld. If there was a criminal library, he'd be the librarian. He may not have your face, but he knows your work."

"How?"

"Because it isn't *his* work. There are only a handful of operators working on his turf. He keeps a finger on the pulse, especially when it might come back on him. He admires your work ethic, your attention to detail and how prolific you've been without leaving clues for investigators." Jase smirked.

"I'm flattered, I guess?"

"If he likes what he sees firsthand, he might be interested in doing some tandem work. Perhaps some solos on your part to distract interested parties away from him. His boss has him headhunting for a capable lieutenant."

"Meh, you know me, Jase." A turtle swiped a piece of food. "I'm not a joiner. I'm doing just fine on my own. Just need a little backup for this one situation."

"Maybe so, but this guy's boss can offer a measure of *protection*… should you need it."

"Do I need it, Jase?"

"Let's just say Mr. White's boss isn't too keen on assassins operating in his AO." *Area of Operation*. "Take one person down he didn't want taken down, and, well—" Jase's fingers made a gun. "—*Pew pew pew*. Safer to be in the fold than out in the cold. Hence, the doss."

"Are *you* working for him?"

"Maybe I am… maybe I'm not. I work for many people. You know how it is for a former action guy. We never truly retire. I'll say this. There are worse bosses out there for you to align with." He threw more food. "The Russians, for example."

"I've got my own network of trusted associates."

"And he has files on them, too."

"Who the hell is this dude?" I demanded.

"Can't tell ya that. TS/SCI kinda shit. Gotta be in to get that info, and getting in isn't willy nilly. The vetting process takes time, and he's not filling a position like a fast-food joint. He doesn't need bodies. He wants top-tier talent, smart, two steps ahead kinda guys. Professionals." He tossed more dog food.

"And for his lieutenant," Jase continued, "he's looking for a guy who's as capable as he is. Someone who can run the show in case anything happens to him. Someone he can trust if he takes a step back from direct leadership, retire from the game."

"Retirement?" My brow furrowed. "Do men like us ever retire? Are we even allowed to?"

"I can't answer that. I don't have the wisdom. For now, he's in search of a ghost of his caliber to work behind the scenes, take some dirty work off his hands so he can focus on… other things."

"Fantastic," I said with sarcasm, realizing my days as a private contractor could end, pissed someone knew about me without me knowing about them. Dog food flung from my hand harder than his.

"Don't sweat it, bro. Just partner up with his wet work guy, Mr. White, for this job, and let the chips fall where they may after it's done. I'm sure you'll know by that point whether it's your jam—if you're still alive. Here's his burner number."

Jase traced the seven digits with his fingertip on his leg, and I memorized the number. No paper trails.

"He'll only answer once, then destroy the phone, so if he's gonna team up with you, that's your only shot. Don't try to convince him. Stick to the facts and don't use your own phone. Get a burner."

"Got it. Thanks, Jase." Just as I stood, Torro erupted from the dark water and snatched one of the two chickens from the dock post. I backpedaled over the bench onto my ass. Jase laughed and smacked the damned alligator on the snout when he breached the surface to get the other one. Torro then crawled up his muddy slide into the grass to sun himself and digest Jase's peace offering.

"He's a pussycat when he's got a meal in his belly." Jase grinned as he mounted the beast from behind, pressed one hand over the dinosaur's eyes, and scratched Torro's neck under those deadly jaws.

"You're nuckin' futs, bro." I shook my head and walked back to the house to retrieve my cell, well clear of crocodile hunter and his *pal*. "See ya!" I shouted over my shoulder.

"Laters, baby. Call if you need anything." Then he did his own goofy impression of the crazy Irish guy in *Braveheart*. "It's my island, aargh."

NINE

I dialed the number from memory. The phone rang once. Before I could say hello, a low, salty voice on the other end said, "The Bar. Ybor City. Thirty minutes," and hung up.

I shattered the phone, separated the battery, and dumped the pieces in a trash can at the gas station I'd just bought the burner from. Then, I removed the battery from my personal cell, tucked it in the glove box next to my Sig, and pulled out to the I-4 on-ramp. *Game on.*

Twenty minutes later, I drove into the rear parking lot of The Bar. As soon as I scooted into a booth in a dark corner, I checked my watch, and waited, satisfied I was early. A pretty little redhead came from behind the bar a couple of minutes later, slid a pair of fireball shots and a Coors Light in front of me with a duck-faced, brow-raised silent challenge. *Kinsley* on the name tag.

"Figured you for a pair of fireballs," she quipped, smirking to herself as she caught me in her little web. I'd never seen a redhead with her coloring. Maybe she was foreign … maybe she was dyed.

"And the Silver Bullet?" I asked, unable to deny my roving eyes.

"Don't drink it if your mountains are blue," she fired off, spun on her heels, and returned to her station behind the bar. Spunky little sprite stacked and stealth. Sure, I'd sworn off the model types because of the ex, but that little woman had something extra about her and she wasn't tall like the ex.

I'd never been to this bar, but I might add this place to my hunting grounds.

With little else to look at besides the day-drinking vets, I watched Bartender Betty making the rounds and bussing tables. Kinsley chatted with a couple of barflies. Smiled a lot. Seemed to give others her full attention. Meh. That one paid attention, too much for a man like me wanting to blend. Too bad.

I'd been so locked onto her I hadn't noticed the straggler slow stepping toward me along the back wall. The tall, messy-haired stranger slid into the booth facing me, and looked me up and down, giving off the gay vibe.

"I'm not the kind of guy you're looking for, pal. I'm waiting for someone, and you're in his seat," I urged.

"Shame." The odd fellow checked his nails. "Seems we're both waiting on someone, but seeing as how we've both been stood up, doesn't hurt to chat in their absence now, does it?"

"I'm not your type." I downed the shots and chased 'em with a swig of beer, intending to get up and move to the bar, and out of this awkward situation.

"Oh, I think you're *exactly* my type… *Eric*." My chin snapped up. *Nobody* knew my real name except my tight-lipped network.

I did my best to hide the turmoil coursing my veins at that moment. He had me dead to rights, and by the satisfied expression he aimed at me, he knew. This must be 'Mr. White'. Images of Bruce Willis as 'The Jackyl' pulled up in my mind. That character played gay to achieve *his* aim, too.

"Mr. White, I presume," I lowered my tone so as not to draw attention. He said nothing, but acknowledged with coy body language, still playing the part.

"So, you wanna get outta here, handsome? I know a more *private* spot to talk dirty."

"As long as you don't get handsy, because I'm a get-to-know-you first kinda guy," I asserted.

At that, I left cash on the table for my beverages, and followed the fruity fella out the back door to the gravel lot, and got into his BMW passenger seat. He took the wheel, and moments later, we headed out on the freeway to God only knows where. I figured I was about to be Dahmered or end up partnered with this person, but probably Dahmered.

We ended up at a run-down, 50s-style cinderblock motel a couple of miles off I-75, where Mr. White backed into a parking space, pulled a briefcase from the trunk, and unlocked the door, ushering me inside. He did a quick sweep for listening devices after closing the door, and opened the briefcase, tossing several file folders on the bed.

"I've seen your work. Clean. Tidy. Up to my

standards. I'm confident in your professionalism. What I need to know is, can I trust you? And I'm sure the same question is looming in your mind," he said. "Take a look."

As I opened the folders, my handiwork stared back. This guy had case files of his own, and from various law enforcement agencies in the region. My throat tightened. This guy could anonymously turn me in and burn my goose to a crisp for the next eighty years. The worst part? I had nothing, *zero*, *zip*, *nada* on him to counter with.

"Not to worry, Eric. I have no intention of burning you. I'm more interested in cultivation. Bringing you on as my understudy."

I balked in my mind, but the evidence was glaringly obvious. He *was* better than me. I wasn't sure about technicality, but at being three steps ahead of the competition, and probably everyone else, I'd met no one as meticulous. Jase was right: Mr. White was a librarian.

"This little mission you're on will be your interview." Mr. White produced more folders, handed them to me, and took a seat in the corner, periodically tipping a finger behind the curtain to peer outside. In the folders was reconnaissance on the Russians. Each of the eight leaders of the Miami Moscovas had a nearly complete dossier with far more information than I'd been able to collect. *Rival criminal enterprises with those of his boss, perhaps? Know thine enemy as thyself?*

Over the next two hours, Mr. White laid out his plan and addressed potential snags, and how to deal with them. This guy was good. Very good. Like a walking flowchart for every potential failure. Immaculately accurate maps and floor plans. This guy had somebody in Miami on the inside of every city and county government office to have this much usable data.

Mutually satisfied that we had a solid plan, we collected our things, and he took me back to The Bar.

"Don't try to contact me. I'll get in touch with you." Mr. White stuck out his hand, not to shake, to display four fingers. "Four days from now, you'll receive a delivery at your door. Accept the delivery, and instructions will be in the package. Follow them to a tee. Don't worry about when you'll see me next. I'll be where I need to be when you need me to be there."

"Yes, sir."

"That's what I like to hear."

I rolled my eyes and waited for him to drive away then got into my beater Ford.

With all he had on me, he wouldn't have difficulty tracking me down. Probably had my personal number already.

I drove off toward St. Pete, but exited, turned back, and headed toward Barks' place. I needed to get him up to speed on everything from the past month, but I needed to see the girl again, too. I couldn't explain or justify why. I just did. Maybe to remind myself why I was neck-deep in this shitty death march.

"Hey, man," Barks said when I jumped out of the truck.

"Yeah, yeah. Don't say a word. I know." I rubbed my shoulder as we walked toward his cabin.

"You know I have no problem helping, it's just with the mission you're on—"

"Barks, I know. Where's the girl? I'll get her outta here.

I get it and you've had her for far longer than we planned. I'm grateful."

"Where are you taking her?" he asked and opened the screen door. "Emily!" he called.

"I can't tell you that." I waited just inside the threshold.

"Good answer," Barks approved.

Emily called from the bathroom that she'd be right out. Barklay lowered his voice near my shoulder.

"Her blood panel came back. No sign of STDs or drugs."

My brows rose in surprise. "She was telling the truth?"

He nodded. "She had to be. You know Ruskies dope 'em and disease 'em."

"Volkov wanted a healthy baby," I said for his ears only.

Barks nodded again. "Since you didn't find a body, I'm betting Volkov got what he wanted."

As a healthy Emily sauntered into the room adjusting the too-long sleeves of one of Barklay's shirts, I was looking right at Volkov not getting exactly what he wanted or else she'd be dead. I'd foiled the boss's plans the day I found her, and I'd never been more pleased to piss on someone's agenda.

"Ghost is taking over from here," Barklay told her. She bit her lip and cast nervous eyes his way. "He's safe. I trust him with my life, now it's your turn."

She pursed her lips and thanked him for taking such good care of her. He allowed her to hug him goodbye, then sent her out the door toward my vehicle. We walked onto the porch, watching her trek across the dirt.

"Dude," I whispered. "Did you…?"

"Bang her?" He balked. "No. Only an asshole would take advantage of a woman in her state of mind." His finger drew circles around his ear. "She's smart, but she's unstable. Be careful out there."

He clapped a hand on my shoulder and wished me luck. Emily and I waved at him, then left this chapter of our journey in the dust of his driveway.

TEN

"Where are we going?" Emily asked after a long period of silence.

"To a safe house."

"You've been gone a long time."

"Yeah. I was working." *On that death wish you told me I had.* "I sometimes travel for business." Though I wanted to tell her what I was up to, I worried I'd give her false hope if I couldn't pull this off. Mr. White was a badass, but I'd never seen him in action. The best laid plans go awry all the time. Sure, he was a walking flowchart of what-ifs and back-up plans, but working with someone for the first time on the most dangerous job of your life was the most terrifying trust fall I'd never known to imagine.

Then, I'd think of the baby. Imagine the little girl cut and ripped from her mother's womb by gruff Russians and I thought of my own parents. Both chronic alcoholics and drug addicts leaving me scrounging for food and shelter while they got their fix. Mom overdosed on heroin; Dad turned me over to the state. I became a boy lost to the system at the mercy of foster parents, most unfit to be around children, much less raise them. I'd have been better off with my dad. He'd passed of liver failure when I was sixteen.

The idea of the baby growing up in an environment where humans were disposable … if I'd endured atrocities as a little boy, I cringed and tried to unimagine what sick fucks did to little girls. I had to save her and preserve her mother to give her the life she deserved. Both of them. Just because I had a shitty upbringing, and her mother was kidnapped and trafficked didn't mean the baby had to suffer the way we did. Maybe wounded souls like ours could find happiness or redemption?

"I need some clothes," Emily broke the silence. "Barks let me wear his gym clothes, and they've been comfortable after surgery and recovery, but I'm losing the baby weight and need some of my own." Emily looked at me instead of the window. "It would be nice to feel like a girl again."

"I can't take you shopping. Too risky. At least until this thing is done."

"What thing?"

Shit. Dumbass! "Tell me your sizes, and I'll do my best."

"What thing?" she pressed harder. When I shook my head, she gaped. "Oh my gosh, you're not—"

"Gonna rescue your baby and take out the entire cell who captured you?" I said too gruffly. "Yeah. That's what I'm doing. What I've been working on for the past five weeks."

She tented her hands in prayer and placed them over

her open lips, then stared out the window, but I don't think she looked at anything.

"If you make a list, I'll hit the store once we're settled," I said quietly.

She answered just as softly. "Thank you."

The safest house I owned was a deer camp a good five miles from the next home and fifteen miles outside of civilization. The only other vehicles to cruise these back roads were logging trucks clearing pine plantations eight miles away. Nature made the only sounds you could hear. Hunting season was over, so the area would remain secluded for another five months.

"Where in the world are we going?"

"Hunting cabin. No cell service. Off-grid." I warned her of the local flora and fauna, including bears, gators, and snakes, but as I laid out my rules, one by one, she agreed.

I'd taken no one to this property. Not even my network would know where to find her. With no wireless in the area, no one could track signals or trace pings from towers to find our location.

We turned off the dirt wildlife management road onto my property. I unlocked the swing gate, drove in, and locked the heavy chain again. As we drove on, the sawgrass, pine branches and palmetto fronds of marshy overgrown entry road brushed and screeched against the sides of the truck. The occasional squish and fling of mud flew up past our windows as we ventured deeper and deeper into the wilderness on the boggy road. Emily held the 'oh-shit handle' with one hand and the dashboard with the other as we slogged through for a half mile to my cabin.

The track told me no one had been out here snooping around, not even hunters. *Good.*

I unlocked the door and held the entry open to Emily. She stepped into the cabin, looking around herself in the dim darkness of twilight. When she reached for a light switch, I winced.

"Off-grid, remember? There's no electricity or natural gas meters here. I have a full propane tank." I pointed out the window to the large tank in the yard. "The fireplace is gas, you just gotta light it and the stove with matches. I'll show you." I took her into the small kitchen and pulled out a box of long matches. She watched me light the flame under the burner, then I told her to try. Took her a few attempts, but she cheered when she lit a flame. I warned her about not blowing up the house leaving the gas going too long before lighting the vapors.

"Fireplace next?" she asked. I grinned with pride at her willingness to do this on her own. My ex-wife was as helpless as they came. At first, I loved her making me feel needed, then she just became needy and unsatisfied with everything I did.

While I watched Emily light the flame beneath the fake logs, I pulled the couch into a bed. "You're a fast learner."

She beamed at me. "Thanks."

I averted my stare at how transformative her face was when she smiled. Even with the constant pain in her eyes, her entire face smiled with her lips, and she looked so soft and kind. Who could ever hurt someone like her?

"You have running water?" she said, brief hint of sarcastic humor. "Or do I have to use a bucket and dump it out the window?"

"Nah. There's an outhouse for that. Tossing it out the window will attract bears."

Her mouth dropped in horror, and I couldn't keep a straight face. When I laughed and told her I was playing, she slapped my stomach with the back of her hand and uttered a giggle. For this tiny moment, she seemed younger. I'd forgotten she was only in her twenties. I was thirty-one.

I cleared my throat. "Fresh sheets and linens are stored in the closet near the bathroom. We have plumbing and running water on a well. The fridge, stove, washer, and dryer are on gas, AKA propane. Deep freeze is full of deer meat on a two-plug outlet linked to a solar generator, but everything else is 1880s fabulous. Candles, matches, kerosene lamps and pilot lights."

"We?" she asked. "Are you married?" She peeked at my hand.

I laughed. "No way. I'm as single as a one-dollar bill, baby. I meant we, the two of us here together, have plumbing and running water."

Jeez. I needed to be careful with my language.

I pointed to the steno pad and pen. "Make that list. I'll hit Walmart." I set about lighting the lamps as darkness descended. Being a Miami girl, I didn't gather she'd spent many nights in a deserted forest. Her finger had to be sore she was writing so much. I went ahead and put fresh sheets and blankets on the couch and the bed in the loft over the kitchen.

I'd just won a battle with the last corner of a fitted sheet when her head poked up from the ladder. "This is so cool!" She climbed the rest of the way until she stood while I crouched. The ceiling was six feet tall at the tallest point where the roof tented over my bed.

"You can have the loft if you want," I offered. "I figured it would hurt your belly to climb up here otherwise I'd have offered sooner."

She peeked at the little built-in bookshelf. "My belly is tender, but Barks made me wear this thing called a binder. It helps. Do you like to read?"

"Nah. Those were here when I bought the place."

She crawled across the bed to the matching bookshelf. "Ha. Looks like a husband and wife. On that side you have westerns. On this one romance."

"Do you like to read?" I asked.

"My mom only allowed educational shows on TV, so I grew to love reading." She traced the tacky titles. "Never read anything like these though." A brief laugh rushed through her smiling lips when she wiggled one of the shirtless covers.

"Guess you have company while I'm gone," I joked. My face grew serious. "I'm about to leave. Stay put no matter what. The shotgun is right beside the fireplace. If anyone other than me comes to the door, shoot first, ask questions later. Locals don't roll up on country homes like these. There's bottled water in the pantry. I'll be back in a couple hours."

A couple hours turned into a three-hour tour of Walmart and Dollar General. Buying feminine products, not my jam. Who the hell knew if I got the correct brand

and type. Felt like I was reading Russian in that aisle. I hadn't even known what breast pads or lanolin were before this humiliating excursion. Breast pumps were hella expensive. Barks hadn't said a damn thing about this stuff. When I called him to ask if she'd used this while she was with him, he said no.

"You told her what you're doing?" he asked.

"Not on purpose. It just, I dunno, slipped out."

"That's what she said." He snickered at his lame joke.

"It's not funny. Some woman told me I was a good husband to be shopping for my wife after having a baby. What do you say to that?"

"I dunno. What did you say?"

"I thanked her then asked her to help me. Of course, she picked the nicest of the nice shit. Good thing I'm not poor."

Barklay guffawed. "I'll say this for ya, Ghost. When you go hard, you give it your all." Barks laughed his ass off. "Can't fuck it up now. She plans on nursing her baby."

"No pressure," I snapped.

Amusement never left his tone. "I warned you not to dig your own grave. All I can do is pray for you now. I'm about to get some after the fast you forced on me. Enjoy celibacy, Daddy."

He hung up on my profanity, laughing all the way.

When I returned, Emily was fast asleep in the recliner by the fire, her thumb between pages 93 and 94 of a Zane Grey novel. I repositioned her blanket to cover her shoulders, removed the book from her hand, and stood taking in her image. Caressing her hairline with my eyes, thoughts of running my fingers through her silky raven hair taunted me as her peaceful slumber lulled me. *Dammit.*

I didn't want to imagine the shit that woman at Walmart put in my head. Men like me didn't have families. I didn't even know this girl.

Why did I suddenly feel guilty about Miami, as if I'd cheated on her? We weren't together, but I hadn't felt this since I left my ex-wife for deployment, *before* I found out she was cheating on me, when love and trust still existed between us. That naïve, first love flutter teased the tatters of my snipped heart strings.

In my head, I imagined Emily just like this with a sleeping infant nestled against her. Was she dreaming of the same?

I broke free of the trance, deciding not to bring the shopping bags in until morning to avoid waking Emily. A cold front moved in. The air chilled enough to keep all the perishables cold. She could have her Christmas morning with a solid night's sleep. Safe. Warm. Cared for. Protected. Not under a bridge bleeding to death.

ELEVEN

"Oh my gosh, what is that amazing smell?" Emily roused with a stretch and a yawn at the bright light of eleven a.m. Fresh-brewed cowboy coffee mingled with heavenly aromas of secret ingredients folded into my omelets. I'd picked up some comfort foods I assumed she might enjoy, including Cuban Empanadas from the bakery.

She kicked the recliner closed and went to the bathroom. I grinned to myself when she thanked me for the products I'd stocked in every spare inch of the tiny lavatory.

When she emerged, I offered a plated omelet with fresh salsa or an empanada. She scoffed and grabbed the plate. "This looks amazing! Barks doesn't make more than coffee for breakfast. I haven't eaten like this since ... well ... since I was free."

When I expected to look at her and see sorrow, I saw her close her eyes during a bite as if savoring the flavor before chewing.

"This is delicious! You're a great cook!" The *mms* and *ahhs* emanating from her made me stand a little taller akin to when I used to draw Mom a picture and she'd place the page under a magnet on the fridge. Before she started using. Like Mom, Emily treated my work like I'd crafted a world-renowned masterpiece.

Flattered by her genuine gratitude, I fought a little blush and sat on the couch to dig into my omelet. When she finished, she thanked me again, then took her plate into the kitchen and ran a little sink of hot soapy water.

"You don't need to do that. I usually do the dishes."

"Of course, you do. You're a loner. Who else is gonna wash them?" she quipped with a little grin. "You can't tell me a hook-up has been crazy enough to come out here with you." She looked around the sparse space. "This is your man haven."

I nodded and ate. She had my number in this tiny way. I gestured with my fork to the bags piled on the tiny two-seater butcher-block dining table. "Sorry I didn't wrap them."

She clapped her hands and darted across the room. Behind me, she rummaged like a little rat, gushing over the supplies, clothing, treats, creature comforts, until her arms choked me with a sudden hug. Her lips blessed my cheek, and she rushed around finding homes for her items like this cabin was her own haven instead of mine.

She was so grateful for the smallest things everyone took for granted. She didn't even complain about the tiny shower like I thought she would. I wasn't sure what to do with my hands. She stole my dishes when I was done eating. Before I could argue, she washed the plate and hummed a song from her head.

"Coffee refill?" she asked, eyes brighter than the pretty day. She was so happy. I couldn't figure her out, so I nodded and let her fill my mug, then I stepped outside to sit on the porch looking over the woods, quietly sipping black coffee.

She poked her head around the door frame about thirty minutes later. "Mind if I join you?"

"Not at all." My foot tapped the additional rocking chair. Emily sat beside me and sipped from her own mug. With all her exuberance, I expected her to chat my ear off, but she found a pleasantly creaky rhythm and watched the birds in the trees like I did.

She left only to grab the western novel and resumed rocking her chair, reading, and sipping. Resolve steeled inside my head at that moment. To answer Jase in my mind, she was worth all the hell to begin in two short days.

"Weather's coming," I said into the quiet between us.

"Oh?" Her eyes remained glued to the novel. "How do you know without TV or a phone?"

I tapped my shoulder. "Clairvoyant since high school football tore my rotator cuff." I squinted at the bright blue sky. "I estimate about dinner time we'll see storms."

"Cozy reading weather, especially beside the fireplace." She turned the page. "You cooking dinner or want me to?"

"I'll cook until I have to leave, because you'll be here to cook your own meals for however long my mission takes." I didn't want to add *if I didn't come back or live through this.*

She paused and peered into my eyes. Thankfully, she simply nodded and accepted my offer to refill her coffee. Throughout our afternoon, we remained like this. I broke down and let her pick a book for me to try. I pretended to read, flipped pages, glanced at the text enough to catch the gist so when she'd ask I'd share accurately. She was proud of me for reading like I was that child again, but she wasn't being condescending. Her happiness was so simple and legit, I couldn't feel insulted.

Besides, she'd picked a romance novel for me with some spicy scenery, so, at least I got mental boob action. After a while, I wasn't fake reading, and I found her silent company quite enjoyable until the first rumbles of thunder stole us from our alternative universes.

The wall clock said I was right in my guestimation. She noted the same aloud and closed the front door behind us.

I made dinner. We cleaned together.

"I'm exhausted," I admitted. "All the heat in that book took the steam right outta me." That earned a little giggle. "Sweet dreams, kid." I patted her head on my way to the ladder. "I'm taking the loft so you can keep reading by the fire." If she needed another world to fall into, I didn't want to disturb her escapism.

"Goodnight," she called. "Thanks again. For everything."

"You're welcome." Though lightning flashed beyond the curtains, I loved thunderstorms. I needed the heavy sounds like mortar blasts and constant battle to lull me to sleep after the war. Quiet was only comforting during the day when my eyes were open. At night, I had trouble sleeping without these sounds. This nightcap was the perfect ending to the most pleasant day.

"Ghost," a voice whispered. "Ghost!" Not a whisper. A panicked cry. "Ghost! Wake up!" Someone was shaking me. I caught my flying arm before I did any damage and opened unfocused eyes on a woman climbing into bed with me. "Oh, thank God you're up! I'm scared!"

Her body pressed so close she buried her face into the crook between my arm and neck. Wind howled across the window screens. Rain pelted the roof so hard I worried the sound was actually hail.

I army crawled toward the little window behind my floor mattress and ripped the curtain aside. Lightning strobed like a Maglite shined into my eyes. I dropped the curtain and blindly pulled the covers over both of us.

"Shh, it's okay. These squalls are normal for this time of year. If we get a tornado, it will be small."

"How can you be so calm?!"

I ran my hand over her hair. "What good is panicking? If it's our time, it's our time no matter what."

"I came up here for comfort, not added stress. Don't talk that way," her muffled mouth chastised against my chest. Desire unfurled at the feel of her lips and breath against my bare skin. Oh, shit. I tried rolling away from her, but she clung tighter like I was being rude.

"If you don't want an indecent proposal, you might want to let go of me."

She froze and understood a little late.

"Ghost, do you think if someone steals your virginity against your will that they count?"

My boner fell flat while my heart clenched. "No, I

don't." Without thinking, I tilted her chin with my nose and kissed her mouth when our lips aligned. Her breath sucked deep, and hands wrapped around my head to pull me back for another.

"Will you take mine?" she whispered while the rain slammed the roof. Somehow, she didn't seem to remember her fear. "I've never been with anyone I wanted before. I want to be with you."

"You don't want to give that to me. It's special."

"So are you. To me. If I get to choose who to give it to, I choose you. Don't make me give it to someone else when you're my choice." Her lips brushed mine again. The heat of her mouth matched the heat of her body pressing closer to mine reviving without a choice. "I've never been kissed … properly. Like with affection or with care."

"Say no more," I said before plying her lips apart to show her what she'd missed. At first, she was timid, untried, which blew my mind, but the more I thought about her words, her reactions, the more I remembered traffickers weren't there for pleasure or affection. They had a greedy need and didn't care if they abused or even killed someone in the throes to fulfill their sick fantasies.

"Please, keep going," she begged. "You taste better than your cooking."

I grinned and gave as she commanded. Her feet pushed at my pajama pants, trying to shove them off my hips, but she got frustrated when I laughed at her failed attempts. She broke our kiss and used her hands. I may have helped before the frenzy that followed. When she said she wanted me, she meant her words and screamed to the rafters from beneath me, on top of me, in front of me, grabbing the curtains and everything in between as she sought her own pleasure for the first time.

Damn if I wasn't having fun in the middle of fornication. How did that make sense? How did lust mix with joy this way? She seemed like she was having fun, too. I hadn't even felt this odd combination when I'd fallen for my ex-wife.

Emily no longer cared about the storms, the winds, or the intense darkness of living without electricity. She didn't complain about anything, and I loved that.

Barks had told me that her milk hadn't come in but that the pump would stimulate her into production. At the time, I'd nearly gagged. I wasn't gagging when I tasted what she thought she didn't have.

Over the remaining time we had together, we only untangled to meet our basic needs like bathroom breaks, coffee and food, then christened every spare surface of the house like newlyweds. She'd gotten so excited to see her milk, she'd cheered, then seemed to remember herself and clam up in shame and embarrassment until I told her I'd already had breakfast long before the light of morning and she'd had nothing to be embarrassed about.

"Your baby has competition," I joked. "You're delicious and I'm newly twisted. Feels like *you* popped *my* cherry."

She'd cackled and grabbed my hair on a long moan when I dove in for another tasty meal. All jokes and joy aside, when the morning came for me to leave, we laid in my bed and she splayed on top of me like her little body could pin me in place.

"Hey, the sooner I leave, the sooner I come back with you baby girl." I stroked her hair and kissed her forehead.

Her face tilted up to catch my lips in hers, but where she'd moaned through so many kisses, she now whimpered.

"Please come back to me. I lost her. I can't bear losing you too if you can't find her. I'll live with the pain for the rest of my life. I …" *love you.*

She didn't have to finish the sentence, nor would I, though I knew I'd fallen for her because this emotion was far deeper and different than anything I'd felt for my ex-wife. In fact, compared to this, I'd surmise I'd never known what love was until this sacrifice. If I stayed with her here, I'd never forgive myself and she could never love me the way she thought. She needed her whole heart, and the baby had the other half.

Despite her protests, I dressed and went out to the truck for my spare pistol, then came back in to give one last goodbye and instructions. "Keep the doors locked and keep this with you at all times. Like I said before, if you see anyone but me on the property, shoot first, ask questions later." I kissed her soft lips, turned and paused at the front door. I couldn't look back. I pulled the door closed, leaned back against the wood for a moment, sucked a deep breath, then fired up the Ford, peeling out and down the private drive toward a destiny of certain death.

TWELVE

S unrise in my rear-view jabbed like a stinging punch in the nose, the kind that makes your eyes water. My sunshine was behind me, sunset ahead, and nothing but night in-between. Darkness filled my mind and soul as I prepared for what was to come. *Get your head in the game or get dead, Ghost. Either way, give 'em hell and send 'em there first.*

Back at my condo, I waited, and waited, and waited all damn day with my cell at the ready, an arsenal in one duffel bag and my mission gear in the other. Just after sunset, a pizza delivery driver with a local pizzeria logo lit on the roof of his car whipped into the driveway, lights blazing through the bay window. The young man, in full delivery guy uniform, quick-stepped two medium pizza boxes up the walkway to my front door. I opened it, pistol in my hand behind the door, accepted the warm pizza boxes, and handed him a twenty for "such a quick delivery when I'm starving."

The guy stutter stepped back to his car and peeled out

through the neighborhood in typical delivery driver fashion. If he was just hired for an extra delivery, he fit the bill.

I closed and locked the door, retreated to my windowless study, and opened the boxes. In one was a manila envelope. Inside was a thumb drive and a simple note.

Happy hunting.
—Mr. White

I plugged the drive into my USB port and imported the docs to my tablet. Not only was there everything I needed to execute the hits but also drop points to pick up gear, room reservations, fake IDs for check-ins and what to expect step-by-step. I didn't even need to bring my own.

In the other pizza box was, well, pizza. If Mr. White wanted to send a message that he knew EVERYTHING about me, he had a unique way of doing it, down to the toppings. Ham, pepperoni, hamburger, black olives, green olives, mushrooms, extra cheese and… jalapenos. Nobody just orders that combination. Considering the timeline Mr. White had in the package, I needed to leave now. Cover of night was likely his reason for waiting until dark to deliver the package all along.

I grabbed my gear bag, just in case what he picked wasn't my jam. Operators are very particular about their gear. I left all but a Bushmaster and a Sig .40 and their silencers in the duffel then stowed the bag in my secret panel under the hallway runner. This time, with high stakes, I loaded up the armored SUV I'd bought at government auction under the auspices of being a private contractor celebrity driver and bodyguard for the rich and famous.

This would be the first time I'd pulled the vehicle out of the garage since I bought it last year, except to wash and detail it every three months. Guns and gear fit into the secret panel beneath the removable console, and with everything secured, including my tablet mounted with Mr. White's directed route displayed, I set the pizza in my lap, a bottle of water in the cupholder, and pulled out of the garage. I kept the headlights off as I idled onto the street until I was halfway through the neighborhood.

On the road, now, the magnitude of what I was about to undertake weighed on me. Over the course of two days, the entire Miami Moscovas would be dead, baby rescued and on her way to her mama, and me? Well, if I survived, probably Mr. White's next target.

I half-believed he wanted the Russians dead to eliminate a vicious rival, but knew he couldn't do the deed solo. The baby was the only sticky point. Scorched earth would've been easier and faster, but the kid added an element of precision that had to be maintained to achieve success.

After retrieving the gear at pre-planned drop points, I headed to the first of three motels to be utilized over the next three days and waited for Phase II as directed by Mr. White. Exactly one hour from my planned arrival time, Mr. White unlocked the door and closed the curtains, scanning for bugs and unloading his duffels into the room.

"Two cars will be delivered tomorrow afternoon for

Phase III. We'll infiltrate in these separately to take down every Russian business front in one night. No boo-hooing if some girls don't make it out alive. Do what you've got to do to eliminate the thugs and stay on track. Timing must be perfect to hit them all, and hesitation from some unfortunate collateral damage is unacceptable."

I nodded.

"Both cars get dropped at my local contact's house, and we move into Phase IV, where you'll drop me off with your SUV, and I'll have over watch on the leaders' safe house through night one and into night two, where you'll set off the knockout gas into the HVAC system, get in, get the baby, and get out. Once you're out, I finish the leaders off and clean-up. I exfil myself. No vehicles. No eff-ups. No diverting from the plan. Meet me back at my contact's safe house at the address in your packet, where we'll move into Phase V, cover story.

"You're my domestic partner, and we'll be living it up in the pink and blue district. Nobody will look for a gay couple if there are any survivors. They will, however, be looking for quick escape pros with their mafia cohorts, eyes and ears everywhere in the Metro area. Let the hunt for us blow over for a couple of days, then ride out together in the SUV. Are we clear?" Mr. White drilled through my brain with the seriousness of his stare.

"Check. No diverting. No fuck-ups. Clean and fast," I assured. "And you're sure the baby's there?"

"Good. Phase IV, Get some sleep. We're sleeping in. There won't be any more until we get back. And, yes, the baby will be there. There's something I have to withhold from you we'll discuss later, as in after we've ex-filtrated with merchandise in hand. No questions until I say so."

"Roger that. And Volkov will be there?"

"I'm betting on it. So is my boss. There's a history there, but that's not your concern. Just focus on your part."

"Copy." I turned over in my queen bed to crash out while Mr. White cleaned his guns and prepped his gear for a couple of hours. Midnight. As tired (and worn out by Emily) as I was, I wished I could stay up later to adjust my circadian rhythm a bit, but I was flat bushed and out cold by twelve-fifteen.

When I woke at nine a.m., Mr. White was nowhere to be seen. The Tesla he'd driven here was gone, too. This made me nervous that I might get hung out to dry by my enigmatic mission partner. I picked up a few groceries at the Asian food mart a block away, including some herbal remedies to revive me with the energy and alertness I'd need for the next two days. When I returned, Mr. White was back.

"Time to move," Mr. White prodded and loaded up his rental.

"On it," I replied. Time hack: four p.m. Next stop, motel number two.

"We're checking in, but we're not moving in. Just get your gear on and ready to roll at nightfall. Leave the keys to the SUV with the front desk for 'Joey' the mechanic. It will be towed to a transmission garage and moved to pick up point for Phase VI exit plan. It'll be where we need it when we need it."

"Good to go," I confirmed, and we took two different

directions, each in our own rental, to reconvene at the rally point following execution of our separate hit plans. *Here we go.*

Over the next eight hours, I took out over twenty Moscovas at four low-end brothel locations, while, presumably, Mr. White was taking out another thirty or so at three high-end establishments with pricey girls and more muscle keeping shop.

He'd take the 'pretty girl' spots since even though my face would be beneath a balaclava and the rest of me covered in body armor, my voice might be recognized as myself by the staff, which could lead to any survivor knowing who to look for. I had been on CCTV after all.

Phase III was by far the most challenging mission I'd ever gone solo on. By the end of the night, I nursed serious bruises from bullet strikes and an ornery bastard who stabbed me twice in the leg before breathing his last breath. Thank goodness for body armor. I'd left a blood trail at that last hit location all the way to the car, but I'd gotten away.

When Mr. White and I reconvened at the safe house, he was none-too-happy about my leg. His contact made quick work of patching me up well enough to continue with Phase IV and gave me an intravenous fluid drip with a little special something to keep me going.

From there, I dropped Mr. White off at the apartment building across the street from the leadership's safe house and rested while keeping tabs on Mr. White's live feed from his infrared penetrating scope.

He'd arranged for the apartment he wanted to be vacated for a week, sending the resident family on vacation in the Caribbean. He had three rooms and windows to gain the best vantage point for taking out any squirters, and since I'd be entering from the back alley, I had that side covered.

Time to initiate approached, and I rolled into position with thirty seconds to spare. Up the fire escape I went. On marked time, I set off the gas cannisters in each of the air conditioning intakes on the roof, waited for effect, then took the roof access down to where Mr. White's scope showed six of them gathered, and a smaller heat signature in a bassinet.

The baby. That left two unaccounted for. I dropped one-hundred-and-eighty-degree night vision goggles over my eyes and proceeded cautiously but quickly down the top flight of stairs, taking out one of the two missing leaders in the stairwell. Gas mask on, I blew the door with a breach charge and entered the penthouse apartment. Everyone was out cold. I stepped around their bodies and laid eyes at last on the treasure in her little chest. Her legs flinched, and she suckled her little fingers while sleeping.

I gingerly lifted her and hastened toward the exit when a searing thud snapped my right hamstring, then another hit my left hamstring, and another through my shooting hand that knocked my pistol across the room.

I dropped to my knees and crumpled onto my back, scrambling to hold the baby with my good hand. The gas-masked leader was the biggest S.O.B. I'd ever seen! Seven feet tall, muscular, pointing his silenced pistol at my face. I rolled to my side and tucked into the fetal position to protect the baby.

This was it. Almost made it, but this is where my story

ended. I closed my eyes and waited for everything to disappear.

Thwack. Thwack. Thwack. Thwack.

I opened my eyes to see the big Russian on his own knees. Both hands shot through. More *thwacks* penetrated the surrounding air, rounds going into the heads and torsos of the remaining six leaders. I pulled my boot knife and buried the blade in the hulking Russian's neck, then sliced across, ending the threat.

I tested my legs. One femur seemed shattered by the bullet's impact. Walking would be nearly impossible, but I still had arms and one wounded but working leg. I pushed to my good knee and tucked her close, prepared to crawl. She screamed against my chest, but I only heard my pulse in my ears. They say a broken femur is the worst pain in the world next to child birth. I figured Emily's birth of this baby in my arm was worse than anything, so I could suck the pain through every gasp as I inched closer to the exit.

"I've got you, mate. Let me have her."

When did Mr. White develop a British accent?

Maybe my pain was making me hallucinate?

Next thing I knew, Mr. White took the baby in one arm and pulled me off the floor in one swift motion. My arm slung over his shoulder, the baby in his other, we descended the stairs. Well, he descended the stairs. I dragged us both down with my bum leg. Nothing appeared to slow this man down.

His back knocked the last door open. My vision clouded, whether from pain or blood loss, I couldn't say. We were down an alley when a cab came out of nowhere. Mr. White tossed me in. The cabby seemed to know Mr.

White, and took quick instructions from him to get me out and to a medic, stat.

"Baby," I whispered, wondering if this was how Emily felt when I came upon her.

"I've got her. She's safe."

Mr. White slammed the door and took off in the opposite direction. The rest of the plan went to shit, but miraculously, I was alive.

THIRTEEN

An associate of Mr. White's retrieved me three days later from the veterinarian who set my leg and patched the damage. The next day, I was back in Tampa, courtesy of Mr. White's boss' helicopter. The pilot didn't take me to a hospital or to Mr. White or his boss. He landed in the field behind my cabin safe house, where two beefy guys ran to the chopper, picked me up and walked me back to the cabin, full leg cast and all.

I didn't recognize the men, but I recognized Emily being held by two more men on the back porch. Several vehicles parked haphazardly about the yard. A couple more guys milled about inside.

A well-dressed man with dark slicked back hair opened the screen door and ushered my carriers into the house with me still in their grip. He instructed them to lay me down in the Lazy Boy, fully reclined.

"Very well," he said. "Release the girl and get into your vehicles."

They did as he said. Emily ran to me, throwing her

arms around my neck, crying hysterically, and trying not to cause pain anywhere else.

The Dapper Dan apparently in charge called on the radio, "Bring the package, please." A faint British accent, vaguely familiar.

A man backed into the front door, slowly turning to reveal 'the package'.

"Oh my gosh," Emily said, voice faint. She stood; hands cupped over her mouth. "Is that …"

Emily stumbled over her own feet running to the package.

The autocratic man chuckled and said, "Easy, dear. One of you needs to walk properly to take care of this baby."

She laugh-sobbed and gently took the infant against her chest. Emily's nose pressed the baby's soft head. We heard her inhaling. "I knew you'd smell like heaven where you came from," she whispered to her child. Her lips planted several kisses to the peach fuzz over the tiny scalp. "I love you so much."

I looked at the first job I was proud of since fighting beside my guys in the war. Her baby was finally in her arms. Mission complete.

"You are free to sit in the car. I'll be out soon," the man said to the one who'd carried the baby inside.

"Yes, Boss." He nodded at us and closed the cabin door behind himself.

As Emily checked her little girl from head to toe, the 'boss' kneeled beside me, took a breath, patted my good arm, and said, "Eric, isn't it?"

"Seems everyone knows my name these days," I challenged, not really sure what would happen next.

"I'm Klive. Klive King," he said in an almost whisper. "At last, we meet. Mr. White speaks highly of you. His word is golden, and if Mr. White has given you the thumbs up, I think you have a bright future in my organization... if you're up for it. If not?" He did the grimace face and kinda sorta hand. "Let's just say it would be much better for your health if you just said yes."

I got the gist. Work for him or pick my cemetery plot.

"Miss Aguaro." He put thumb and finger together as if to tip his imaginary fedora and bid her adieu. "Take good care of my friend here, Tessa. I look forward to his answer."

She gasped, and the blood drained from her rosy cheeks.

"How did you ...?" Her voice faltered before she found a stronger tone. "Answer? What is the question?" she quizzed, confused.

Klive smirked, tapped his temple, and chuckled as he hit the threshold, turned, and said, "Shame we had to leg it before Phase VI. Woulda been knees up."

Holy shit! Mr. White! Klive King *was* Mr. White!

"Wait. What about Volkov?" I asked. Klive King stopped in his tracks, put his hands in his slacks pockets and paused. "Did we get him?" I asked.

"Don't you mean... Olga?"

"Are you shitting me? *She's* Volkov?"

"Told you Volkov was cagey. Let's just say the Miami Moscovas are finished. I look forward to working with you... Ghost. Get better, now. By the way... just thought you'd want to know in case you were mulling over remaining an independent contractor… you've been on my payroll since your first job. You just didn't know it. What say cut the charade and make it official?" He smirked. "There's a nice little starting bonus on the porch."

With that, King exited and hopped on his chopper, disappearing into the distant sky. In front of the house rested my SUV, my Jeep and the F-150 with trailer and boat attached. They knew where I lived. Probably all my properties. If I said no, there would be no escape or evasion.

On the mantle over the fireplace, I saw a piece highly out of place. Not mine. I asked still-weeping Emily to hand the silver platter to me. She rested the fancy tray on my lap, revealing three items. A ring with small amethyst and onyx stones in the middle of a fleur-de-lis. A bouquet of purple nightshade flowers. And a square, plain black business card with a puff of smoke on one side.

Holy shit. I am so fucked. Nightshade Syndicate. And I was working with the damn boss. Guess I passed the interview?

Beneath was a little welcome card with a personal note in fancy handwriting that assured me with Nightshade I was now free to move wherever I wanted in the light of day because the syndicate had my back, and my family's. My family?

No more hiding.
- K. K.

I looked up in time to see the rest of the vehicles roll out in unison, and all was quiet again …

"What's on the porch?" I asked without looking away from the platter. I almost didn't want to know, but Emily cried out when she went to the door. Several curse words flooded from her lips, and she yanked like she'd forgotten how to turn a knob. I tried moving from the chair, but the door was open, and Emily had the arms of two people wrapped around her. "What the?"

They were crying. All of them. Emily held the baby, and they held her. That's when I realized. She held her baby. They held theirs.

Dammit, Klive King. My eyes filled with tears against my will. That bastard. He was a good boss and bought loyalty through love instead of pain.

Emily pulled away from them and beckoned them into the small living room. "These are my parents," she said through a voice choked with happy tears. Their names would become more familiar to me over the coming weeks but went in and out during her introduction.

She kneeled beside the chair and placed the baby in my arms. Bright blue eyes studied my face, and I was officially weak in the knees though I couldn't exactly stand.

"I should introduce myself," Emily said. "Emily was the name they gave me. Contessa is the name my parents gave me, but I've always gone by Tessa, and this is … Lily Hope." She tucked the baby's blanket closer. "We are so happy to meet you." Her voice broke before she kissed me.

I extended my wounded hand, hoping she'd grasp the

LYNESSA LAYNE & A.J. LAYNE

significance of me giving her my weakness. She took my cast.

"I'm Eric and I'm honored to meet all of you."

Though her parents were a mite confused, Em—er, Tessa, filled them in. I'd never met a more gracious family or felt a part of any family until now. And I owed Klive King for this new life he'd given me and helped me give to all of them.

Tessa smiled and kissed my lips. Define irony: I finally felt safe to put my heart in the hands of the stranger I knew better than anyone. I'd do it all over again, which was good since Klive King wouldn't accept anything less.

Also by Lynessa Layne

The Don't Close Your Eyes Series

Killer Kiss

Don't Close Your Eyes

Complicated Moonlight

Mad Love

Dangerous Games

Hostile Takeover

Target Acquired

Point Blank

Novellas

The Getaway

Magazine Articles

The Villains of Romantic Suspense

ABOUT LYNESSA LAYNE

Lynessa Layne is a native Texan from the small town of Plantersville. She's a fan of exploration, history, the beach (though she's photosensitive), Jesus, and America too (RIP Tom). Besides being an avid reader, she's obsessed with music of all types (hence her reference to Tom Petty). As a child, she created music videos in her mind and played Barbies perhaps a little longer than most with her little sister, not yet realizing she was writing and enacting stories all along.

Though she's put away the dolls, she now uses her novels as an updated, grown-up version of the same play.

Lynessa also co-hosts TropiCon Book Expo & Writing Convention with her hubby, A.J. in St. Augustine, FL and Branson, MO.

She's a member of Mystery Writers of America and River Region Writers, with work featured by Writer's Digest and Mystery and Suspense Magazine.

In 2022, she was a finalist for Killer Nashville's Silver Falchion Awards for Best Suspense and Reader's Choice for Dangerous Games, volume 4 of her Don't Close Your Eyes series, and in 2023 won the Silver Falchions for Best Suspense and Best Book of 2022 with volume 6, Target Acquired.

Sign up for Lynessa's newsletter,
Lit with Lynnie, at lynessalayne.com

Follow her on social media:
facebook.com/authorlynessalayne
instagram @LynessaLayne
twitter @LynessaLayne
tropiconbookexpo.com

ABOUT A.J. LAYNE

A.J. Layne is a native Texan, a 24-year military veteran with over thirty deployments and spin-ups, five combat tours in the Middle East, 268 combat missions, and military advisor roles in a dozen foreign nations during his career. Growing up a military brat, he's used to never staying in one place for long, and has experienced 34 countries and 45 states between traveling with his father's and his own military careers. His myriad misadventures have included working cattle, timber and crops on his family's Texas ranch, getting knocked out trying to ride his uncle's prize breeding bull ('Big Red', a 1,600-lb. monster with a particularly nasty disposition), breaking in broncs, falling off a mountain, being pinned against a coral wall by a passing submarine 60 feet below the surface while free-diving (no tanks) with SEALs in Guam, and being bitten by just about every creature above and below sea level, including a mako shark, a copperhead, a whole nest of redbacks, and even a flock of cheeky geese. Adventure has been in his blood from a young age, as well as venom from a variety of poisonous critters around the world. He found 'fun' in catching rattlesnakes, copperheads and cottonmouths with his boyhood friends, and has sought out evermore harrowing challenges throughout his life – just to see if he could master them. He lives by the mantra, "if you get the opportunity to do something, do it. You may never get the chance again." He describes himself as 'too dumb to die'.

A.J. has been a sports fanatic since he was a tot, and is a life-long St. Louis Cardinals baseball nut, though he sucked at baseball himself. Personal athletic success came in other sports as played rugby for 12 years at the semi-pro level, including two full seasons for Texas-Pan American in the NCAA (two conference titles and an appearance in the NCAA regional championships – lost to Arizona State (the eventual national champions that year), two appearances in the U.S. Military World Rugby Championships [played multiple positions for the Pensacola Aviators], the Amateur Rugby B-Side World Championship (lost in the World Final by two points to Argentina as a wingback for the Washington Renegades [D.C.]), two Australian National Gridiron Premierships in American football (28-0 in two seasons [1996 & 1997] for the Adelaide Breakers – the first national title for any Adelaide-based pro team), fought a UFC champion to a draw in a 5-round exhibition match as a military MMA fighter, redshirted for the Arkansas Razorbacks football team his Freshman year in college [1990-91], and won state championships in football and wrestling while in high school.

Since retiring from military and civilian careers, A.J. now pursues the challenge of a relatively less danger-infused life with his wife [Lynessa Layne] and five children in Alabama, though his misadventures with wildlife continue. He loves camping, fishing, hunting, survival challenges, snorkeling and anything outdoors. He pulls from his real-life adrenaline-fueled experiences to sprinkle reality into his fictional characters and stories to express the 'real feels' that put you in the center of the action, passion, mystery, suspense and risks his characters pursue head-on. Many of his characters' lives are based on his own, and their stories need to be told. This is why he writes.

57908655R00066